GOOD NIGHT, PAUL

For Charles Hood,
a good morning —
special & Rose

with love, or above

Bob Peters

10 Jan '92

Good Night, Paul

Poems by Robert Peters

GLB Publishers   San Francisco

FIRST EDITION

Published in the United States by
GLB Publishers
P.O. Box 78212, San Francisco, CA 94107 USA

Cover Design by Timothy Lewis

Publisher's Cataloging in Publication
(Prepared by Quality Books Inc.)

Peters, Robert.
  Good night, Paul / poems by Robert Peters.
  p. cm.
  ISBN 1-879194-06-6

  1. Poetry--Collections. 2. Love--Poetry. I. Title.

PN6110.L6.P4 1991   808.81
                                      QBI91-1713

First printing, December, 1991
10 9 8 7 6 5 4 3 2 1

For

PAUL TRACHTENBERG

Life-Mate

and for our third decade together

The film GOOD NIGHT, PAUL, a silent five reeler directed by Walter Edwards, was released in 1918. It was based on a successful stage play with book and lyrics by Roland Oliver and Charles Dickson, and with music by Harry B. Olsen. In the early 1970's, the author presented Paul Trachtenberg with the poster for the film.

Thanks to Sophia Corleone, owner of this extremely rare poster, for sharing it with us.

Robert Peters has come a long way from his impoverished beginnings in rural Wisconsin. With a series of impressive academic degrees, he has taught in Universities from coast to coast, has published both scholarly and literary prize-winners, and has been the recipient of several major fellowships. He has also written and acted in numerous performance versions of some of his works, and has a reputation as a feisty, energetic, and responsible critic of poetry.

Peters lives a rich and private life with his lover and companion of nineteen years—poet Paul Trachtenberg, the "Paul" of *Good Night, Paul*.

BOOKS BY ROBERT PETERS

Poetry

FOURTEEN POEMS
SONGS FOR A SON
THE SOW'S HEAD AND OTHER POEMS
EIGHTEEN POEMS
BYRON EXHUMED
RED MIDNIGHT MOON
CONNECTIONS: In the English Lake District
HOLY COW: Parable Poems
COOL ZEBRAS OF LIGHT
BRONCHIAL TANGLE, HEART SYSTEM
HAWTHORNE
CELEBRITIES: IN MEMORY OF MARGARET DUMONT
THE PICNIC IN THE SNOW: Ludwig II of Bavaria
IKAGNAK: The North Wind
BRUEGHEL'S PIG

Criticism

THE CROWNS OF APOLLO: Swinburne's Principles of
    Literature and Art
PIONEERS OF MODERN POETRY (with George Hitch-
    cock)
THE GREAT AMERICAN POETRY BAKE-OFF: First,
    Second, Third, and Fourth Series
THE PETERS BLACK AND BLUE GUIDES TO CURRENT
    LITERARY PERIODICALS:
    First, Second, and Third Series
PETERS VISITS W. S. BURROUGHS (privately printed)
HUNTING THE SNARK: A Compendium of New Poetic
    Terminology

Editions

THE LETTERS OF JOHN ADDINGTON SYMONDS (with
    Herbert Schueller)
AMERICA: JOURNAL OF A VISIT (by Edmund Gosse)
THE POETS NOW SERIES OF LIVING AMERICAN POETS
    Scarecrow Press
LETTERS TO A TUTOR: The Tennyson Family
LETTERS TO H. G. DAKYNS
AUSTRALIAN POETS (the best of *Poetry Australia.* Edited
    with Paul Trachtenberg)

*Please see the end of this book for
additional titles and availability of
other works by* Robert Peters.

ACKNOWLEDGEMENTS

A number of these poems, in earlier versions, have appeared in the journals. I am grateful to the editors.

Black Buzzard, Orange Coast Review, Rohwedder, Rhododendron, Orange Coast Review, Poetry Motel, Blind Date, Archives Newsletter: University of California at San Diego, Pearl, Elephant Ear, The Sculpture Gardens Review, Downtown News, Urbanus, And Magazine, James White Review, Coal City Review, the Tansy Press, Couples Who Are Poets, Redstart Eight Plus, The Kindred Spirit, Stance 5, The Signal, and Sepia 35 (UK).

We thank Noel Lloyd, of Harleston, Norfolk, England, for permission to use the cover collage he adapted from a drawing by Albrecht Dürer of William Blake's drawing for *For The Sexes: The Gates Of Paradise.*

TABLE OF CONTENTS

MONARCH BUTTERFLIES IN NOVEMBER:
SOUTHERN CALIFORNIA

1.

Fluttering over the street,
above the trees, in a corridor,
as the fog erases the sun
its yellow doors and windows close.
Mid-afternoon.

From their insanity, what false summer?
Who opens their chrysalides,
miraculous froth or spume
falsifying itself?

They dive and flutter.

2.

They are mating now.
Two float past, attached.
I think they are mating.
Eggs in their bodies,
small jellied ice-drops,
crystal embryo congealing.

3.

The red cat, its tongue
hoarfrost, slaps them and swallows.
He curls at my feet.
Neither do I eat him,
nor do I beat him.
He is winter.

1

CALIFORNIA PARK: EARLY MORNING

A full moon drips strands of mist.
Dense fog soaks my wrist.
Cats hunker.
They've devoured Easter rabbits
and the ducks maundering the slough.

The early hour charms—that must be it,
the cadence, the thug's step and toe,
the knife at the throat,
Beauty's ocean laved with ice,
hot blood, cold wax, resonance.

BLUE EGGS ON MY TABLE

Birds in yolk, albumin, and water.
No warmth in a chilled house.

One egg loves
a plaster Mexican Jesus.
Blood bathes the gem.
The foetus quickens.

Egg two is yours,
tumescent, spent, addled, flayed.
Your semen shoots
and no one takes it.

Egg three is a fire.
Tie it to your throat.

In a cypress tree
parrots scream.

What's lost may never be found.
What's found will be lost forever.

GEOMETRIES

The red-toned azalea, rose,
the puce convolvulus,
the trailing ants
intent on the mad geometry
raving in the kitchen.
Such cheer and such sobriety!

Despite the gaps, style makes our living easy:
the fatal furnace clank,
the car's camber to the left,
the spider in the ferns,
insomniac drips of rain,
tears, a biceps-stroke, a kiss.

THE GARDEN

A lion growls at a rose
and is calmed. A stork
concocts a nest
on the highest rock.
Deer recline in the shadows.
A silver heart.
Nude men and women
dance around an orange tree.
The ladies wear chokers.
The men tie mistletoe
to their balls. There is a stream
for languorous swimming.
A wall of ivy and wisteria.

Not a fuschia drops.
He and she are linked.
There is ichor, which they drink.
The lion yawns.
Can you prove this false?

THERE'S PAIN IN GARDENING, AS THERE IS IN
POETRY

Those aphids sucking your whorled
rose buds, the mildewed leaves,
the bronzed petals, the rust-sifts
resembling burnt cicada shells,
the enormous green hopper chomping
vertiginous paths through the leaves.
These could drive one from floriculture
to weaving tapestries.

You shake dust, jet-spray poison,
rive the hopper, feed the bushes sulphate,
zinc, crushed oyster shells.
Yet, O Rose, thou art sick.

LEAF HOPPER

Was it a miracle
the gross leaf hopper?

You beheaded him with a trimmer:
the mandibles kept twitching
in the redwood chips.
The body spun in a frenzy,
ramming a window sill.
He swept past your shoe,
wiped his legs fastidiously
and died.

THE SKINTLED GARDEN WALL

Your essentials: trowel, cement mix,
brick. The plumb line follows
the grain until the wall curves up
in a high baroque, non-American twist.

No more termite-riddled wood,
apostrophes of terrace plank
for retaining the soil, eaten paper-thin,
syllables of weeds, thirsting
honeysuckle verbs, passion vines.

TOADS

They were saucer-sized, with
hams and carapaces struck
with topaz carbuncles and emerald
pupils. They usurped the garden,
the broccoli, the malformed cucumbers.

In scooped-out portions of cement block
they fell in on one another,
huge toads piggy-backing,
foul-smelling, urine bleached.
Yet, no sex business that I could see.
I flooded them with a hose.

They leaped forth seeking shade,
their pork-rind jowls gelatinous.

This was the year moth larvae burrowed
into enormous cabbages, cannibalizing themselves.
This was the year our plums nourished
the neighborhood, the year you sang,
the year we bought a new door.

IN THE PARK

Jump. Thrust your legs over the bar
securing the gym rings in Kiddies' Park.
Grab on and angle downward.
Turn your face this way.
Now, hit the sandpile!

There's no false armor here,
no supermarket dross, poisoned apples,
disgrace notes, ravished damsels, pennants
from lost battles, no snivelling Lancelot.
Licorice stems secure your kingdom.
Swing, spin the world on its head.

LOUIS FOURTEEN

1.

Termites
burrow through the fake lintels
I set up as cave dividers.

Longing,
like Louis the Fourteenth,
has entrails twice the normal length.
He ate nineteen courses today.

2.

I pile leaves outside the door.
I eviscerate a rabbit,
slap the wet rib-sides to my face,
and taste God.

3.

I leave for the valley.
Smoke drifts from cottages.
I make love to the first heifer I see.
Her udder feeds me.
I build a house of her dung.
Her hairs are my mattress.
I hope she'll have my calf,
a miscarriage a month!

4.

More?
I do love hummingbird throats
and camellias ready to unfold.

I think of maggots.

Waves jostle.
Everything assumes its opposite.

ON THE BEACH

Near dawn, a shrieking sea gull
is a cello scraping tunes
in an old folks' home.
Nary a dog stirs. The tide persists.
Yellow pier light is phosphorescent.
Oil rigs glisten.

When I left the house for the jetty,
you were asleep.

A dead seal: an open mouth as a white heart,
pink froth, a gunshot wound.
I circle him then proceed south.
Exhilaration, yes.
Salmon clouds. Morning. Rain.
Loving you.

LOVE SPEECH

A white hare
nibbles the nasturtiums.

A neighbor's pit bull
masticates his sinew
floating a fur cape over his ears.

NEARLY MORNING

My flannel comforter
is as warm as yours.
(Are you sleeping on your side?)

In my dream a stubby man
grinds a knife against his jugular,
spews forth neither blood nor rage,
though the slice is keen.
He was in a deep stone well
and draws himself to the lip.
I hear his cry.
Ivy springs from his fingers.
"No!" I shout.

LOVE POEM

He is the essence of aspic,
a flowering honey bee.

Fork tines in pairs,
dozens on a single stem.

Friends in bloody dharmas—
mine as well as yours.

SHADOWS SHIVER NEAR A DOOR

Yes, Charlie strolled with his fat mom,
sipped coffee with his dad,
bought a condo, and clanked along.

Dennis preferred jiggling boy coconuts
on Waikiki to his inhalation therapy.

Ann tootled her Karman Ghia to the beach.
Dennis held your balls while you pumped Ann
on that tacky divan.

And the Christian Science reader
with the lupine hair and the ski sweater
enticed you into his hot tub.

Steve lived at the back, drained phlegm
through an overflow pipe. I died, he said,
extending a hand, crushing a blue moth
with AIDS on its wings.

GARY

He kept himself dangling from the telephone.
He would retrieve the missing cufflinks
tieing him to what was tender.
He tossed his head back
as blood gushed over his teeth.
For he had lied.
The next morning he climbed a mountain,
shot himself, died, and was retrieved
by Air Force men from the nearby base.
He should have fought back, you said,
since he was so exorcised. You pointed
towards the schist where he crashed.
He'd always craved death, something
about an uncle who willed him a watch.
Moreover, it was easy not to fight
dancing to Grandma's house.
He loved the greasy base ball bat
shoved up his ass by the photographer.
He ate mustard, stoned,
and had his cock ridiculed in that porn flick,
as *Michael Tremor*, a sick joke.
Life, he said, isn't always Cracker Jack.
He grins from a eucalyptus tree.
"We remember you," I say.
He rejoins the shades.
A naked snapping in the mist,
a jiggling in a palm, high up
where spidery hairs inseminate dates.

HIPPIE TAILORS

How mellow!
They nestled under an eider down,
chortling Urantian affections,
the sweetest hyssop,
fashioning far-out smocks
for beach homosexuals.
Great dope.
They required a shop.

Yes, joss sticks flopped on our kitchen table
invoked ruby-throated Astarte:
our nest would be theirs!
Our brass front door key melted in the lock.

One fetched a treadle sewing-machine
and bolts of cloth. The other
draped himself in a robe of pyramids,
dismissed our couch,
typewriter, books, your old Chevvie.
"Come inside and play," he beckoned.
"Yes," said the other, "shift to a higher ledge
where the orioles are."

We phoned the police.

19

A TENSILE METAPHOR

Before they're crushed, rouse those lovers.

Yes, I know, they suck and pump, oblivious
to fate's raunchy snap.

Don't feel too sorry:
love is always better
on a mattress in the street.

Here come the claxons!
Two blaring ambulances.
There's no time to explain.

THE WRITER

Pressing his etui strap
between thumb and forefinger
mouthwash in hand

convinced that all bronzed
beach lads have
sanitized armpits

that poems are match flashes
bleached by sun and hot sand
that he is famous (hadn't he

visited that writers' colony
in Portugal?) was invited
to venues to read his work.

When tight bleached jeans
and cowboy boots were in style
he sucked in his gut and preened,

a Ken doll, a chicken hawk
with breast thrust forward,
not a nostril hair displaced.

Earlier his image was preppy.
Now he clog dances
flipping his wrists gaily,

moving in the svelte manner
of Lombard in furs
crossing the parquet towards Charles Trenet.

There has to be more than
minimal wage rock record clerks,
hotel desk pages, bookstore boys.

We always knew he'd despise us.
Affection portages hate.
Hate's there when it's needed.

THE VISITING TENOR

1.

We found an old-fashioned barber,
rotund, with handle-bar mustache,
a bloody butcher's apron, and a diamond
in his right ear lobe.

2.

Near California's Salton Sea
we abandoned the tenor
who had clasped our waists
while chomping gluttonously on dates.
He swallowed the pits. Finally
when he had to pee, we drove off
indifferent to his survival skills
in those desert wastes.

3.

In Julian, we found a barber shop
in a ramshackle building.
I needed a trim.
You misunderstood, I think,
pressured by our guest's slippery farts
as he relaxed in my recliner
pontificating over Caruso, Bjerling,
and Melchior, clipping hair from his nose.
He'd sing for us if we chose.

4.

The barber was from Marseilles,
a city we'd sped from
when we saw feces in the sheets.
He wasn't to blame for our French disaster.
Wisps of my gray hair, silky, like my dad's,
flew to the floor.
You were thumbing *Mad Magazine.*
I scratched my psoriasis.

"You will fetch him, won't you?
He's a regular customer."

"That'll do," I exclaimed, tossing
the hair cutting sheet to the linoleum.
The trimmer smelled of chloroform.

You were counting cigars by the door.
You sang an aria from "La Boheme."
An enraged, sunburned visage.
Tentacles, suction cups, glued to the window.

LOVE POEM FOR WALT WHITMAN, AND FOR YOU

"On all sides prurient provokers stiffening my limbs,
Straining the udder of my heart for its withheld drip..."
         —Walt Whitman, "Song of Myself"

"But O the ship, the immortal ship! O ship aboard the ship!
Ship of the body, ship of the soul, voyaging, voyaging,
voyaging."
         —Walt Whitman, "Aboard At A Ship's Helm"

1.

Old haymaker
rushing to fetch the hay
before the storm
pulps your barley and rye to mash
and ruins your alfalfa crop.

You claimed two oceans at once:
time-urchins tearing off
scraps of land
to stuff their craws.

You fashioned keen machines,
produced transcendental steam
from body cotter-pins and gears,
swung the tongue on a pivot,
hung the phallus on a spring,
the eyes on silver bearings
the breasts and thighs on swivels.

The udder of your heart
withheld its drip
when it was threatened.

2.

Your perpetual high:
did you drink emeralds?
dandelion wine?
Who washed your groin with liquor
brewed from cedar boughs?
your lips with honey?
What incense stunned your system?
What lost health food nurtured you?

I think of pickle brine,
of ambrosia sipped from divine dixie cups,
of cheese pressed from unicorn milk,
of grape juice spiked with cream of tartar.

3.

And your fantasies:
the throat freed of its collar,
the clothed arm undressed,
the belt unhooked and dropped,
the foot made lovingly shoeless.

A hundred bodies clamber laughing
onto the Soul's ship,
onto the ship of the body!
O ship aboard the ship!
They speed gaily away,
leave us on shore, Walt,
on fire-sand with briars and cinders.

4.

The one we love
moves continually inside us,
sits, lies down, lusts, sleeps,
is sometimes satisfied.

He is a beautiful Adam,
she a serene Eve.
They gather us in, stroke us,
bring toes and fingers erect.
Seminal waters rise in the root.

5.

The gay ship glimmers,
a flamingo in the dark.
I no longer hear
its perfumed gears and pistons
creating Cytherean music.

I leave the beach
and take up a stone
softened, shaped
by the sea's pounding currents.

I press the stone to my throat,
the hot small breast of a molting wren.

With speech
we flood the miniature worlds
we seek to decipher,
flood them with acid and brine.
Perhaps, as you said, Walt,
we are flecks of light.

But look!
Over that hill
shaped like the warm groin of a lion
    He walks
    He is walking towards the sea!

BEACH LUST

Binoculars: naked surfers
in one another's arms
half-hidden by van doors.
Wet-suits slicked with kum,
waxy muscular posteriors,
groin muscle, bronzed music,
cacophony of nestled testicles,
arpeggios of zitless pecs,
the bourdons and tympani of sex:
you drive home shaking.

TORSO

His nipples resemble apricots.
His biceps are sheathed,
forearm turned palm up, vulnerable,
sinew attached to bone, etcetera.

By not flirting, the glissando of his speech
rings both with sex and the nature of God.

You crave his image, waft him
through wood smoke, distress, and jagged glass.

GAY FILM

Being in James Broughton's film
was like singing to a Hepplewhite chair
secured by colored ribbon.

Nude (or nearly so)
we lifted weights on the patio.
The camera winked.
You sat on my belly, as directed,
as I lay prone on a workout bench
holding the bar parallel to my chest.

We never called it sport, for who
could have cared less.
I feared, of course,
that fat would smother my jockstrap,
that my turkey wattle chin would show.

Your coppery hair flew in the breeze.
Your muscles complemented mine:
the brisk tenor and the scraggly bass.

THE LAST PICTURE SHOW

The celluloid sizzles,
 the frames liquefy,
a Rosicrucian sepulcher explodes.
Some other way, then.
Throw it all on, amen.
Torch the camera, the megaphone,
the jodhpurs.
 Your violet arm
and inflamed coccyx
are entr'acte and coda,
for the gross 'nineties.

GOOD NIGHT, PAUL

In "Good Night, Paul" Constance Talmadge
arranges her peach-toned negligee
so that the sparrow breast throb of her pulse
winks through the chiffon and seduces Edmund Lowe
before the night and the wine sour.
She's a vamp. She loves the script.
Her tight blonde curls prick her cheeks.
She wears a rhinestone clip and stiletto heels.
Lowe has taped his foreskin,
nestling the excess in cellophane.
Raising her glass Talmadge squeals.
A lipstick flash. The tip of her tongue
is a little hatless man in a boat.

Each night, thumbtacked to your door,
her poster, smiling, tucked you in.
The mint on your teeth, your body in the sheets,
the whoosh of rain, the carp pond flashing fins.
On your move to another town,
you junked the poster, and now
there are no copies, at any price.

Though vaporous, Talmadge remains,
yes, raising her long-stemmed glass,
clicking her heels, caressing her silky haunch:
"Good night, Paul."

SHOPPING PLAZA

In that hermetic cathedral
among the blue-haired, liposuctioned ladies
with their white bags, tennis shorts,
and luminescent leathery eyes,
among the men in tight designer jeans,
kids plunging over bronze bears
near the squealing carousel.
All is "heart," you say,
the Muzak and the potted trees
dripping dust-free leaves.
There's even a stream
of ripened wheat flowing
towards floods of health-bread,
non-cholesterol cookies,
fat-free croissants.

CHRISTMAS

The tree strung with red apples,
snowflakes, the lights,
the shopping trips,
the mediocre holiday films—each one
a partridge in its pear tree,
Godiva chocolates,
trips through the neighborhood,
electronic life-sized teddy bears,
gingerbread, multi-colored house-wrap
whipped off the nails by winds,
light-pole candy canes, the "Chipmunks"
retailing carols, ersatz icicles,
the old tin Coca Cola Santa
positioned near the weepy image
of lascivious wise men.
Joseph amazed.
Much rime in the California light
sparkles on dichondra lawns all night.

My Wisconsin boyhood: wind
rattling the stove pipe, thrumming guide wires.
And the single orange, the apple, the ribbon candy,
the bland coloring books, the wool socks,
the tree fetched from the woods, on skis.

Here, in California, the season
is whisker-brushed by mice nibbling frankincense.
Shampooed dogs dream of basset hound Saint Nicks
loaded with Kibbles and Gravy Train.

Chiffon snow sifts the roof.
At 2 a.m. the prancing of hooves
and a mighty *ho ho ho*.

THE MIRROR NEVER LIES

To see where the fat slaps your navel
is to see less than the factor
of what you are, as an obsession.

Someone earlier scribbled obscenities
warning you not to read in blown sand
the news you dread: adiposity

is where we expect it, in lard,
in nerves and tissue,
in sagging eyelids nurturing phlegm.

Please, turn the mirror to the wall.

GRANDMA

Rage
overpowers her homespun skirts, her plaited hair.
She's lost a screw for a bamboo window blind.
She wants to trench zinnias
but can't find a spade. And where
are the keys for the Dodge
and the silver urn for tears
(memento of Margaret Dumont,
dowager of the Marx Brothers movies)?
Huddled on a braided rug, Granny convulses.

She stops sobbing. She rises. There's
the urn dumped of the heart ashes
of Dumont's favorite chihuahua!
She finds the key and the spade.
"Thank God," she exclaims, jerking a hair
from her nose. Then, on to the kitchen
where butter is softening—chocolate chip
cookies for her grandson Paul.

MAD KING LUDWIG

You perfume Cosa Rara, the King's white stallion
whose withers excite him to a fervor.
You own a gingerbread house lavish
with honey-colored balcony,
geraniums, gentians, and sweet Alpine air:
gifts of the monarch.

Your King saunters through a village,
burnt candle in hand,
his lederhosen open.
The air reeks with wood smoke.
Snow-laden spruce branches flare
with blood-black edges.

His underpants are soiled.
Scour them.
Yes, and his foul lust-cloths.
You must whiff his black teeth
crammed as they are with rancid venison.
You are his man.

THE PLAY BEGINS

In the dressing room
you check my costume, the make-up,
and my glued eyelashes.
"Be direct not emotive," you say.
You line my eyes, cross-hatching them.
I imbibe odors the King fears:
horse blood, human urine,
fecal matter, weasels sucking his jugular.
He beats his scaly fists
on a Meissen porcelain swan.

BAVARIA NEEDS HIM

The King's robe
frays at the neck—the effect
is of a purple hound riddled with mange.
He trips over his gold caftan
which sags over his paunch,
and, with scissors in hand,
in dim candle light, inspects the robe,
then orders a throne
from which he lambastes an architect
for creating arabesques, *not* Gothic pillars.
He dismisses his cousin Sophie
from his betrothal chamber
and seduces a groom.

Your threads stitch his public self
into place. He must not
batter himself on the scenery
or collapse like a fat trout
in the middle of a speech
delivered with opprobrium and disgust.
He recites lines extolling
the loins of his naked soldier lover.
Bavaria needs him, you say,
as does Richard Wagner, as do we.

THE FATIGUED KING

1.

The king fatigued
props himself against the inner wall
of a bulbous Moorish tin kiosk
where he has sapped himself groping soldiers.
The soiled depressions
in the obese Turkish pillows dismay him.
For he repels the men.
When his mustache brushes a buttock
or his jewelled hand hefts a scrotum
the men swirl as if his sucking
were a joy. After all, these peasants
long ago threw off swaddling clothes.

2.

Below, in the stage pit
where the espresso percolates
and the bean sprout salads wait,
a red stereo system glows.
You look up, script in hand
as I shout swan death-songs,
then rip off my black wig.
My eyes are Ludwig's. And, yes,
the actor, too, fears death stench,
as does the author,
as does the King.

POET CELEBRITIES: OUR OVER-NIGHT GUESTS

Some guests were buzzards, cockroaches,
shit-stainers, gossips, spitting coral snakes,
birds of paradise.
Some arrived early and stayed late.
Some were affectionate. Others were acerbic.
Some brought lovers. Others came alone.
A few were celibate. Some splashed cologne
and abused the telephone. Some had bad stomachs,
viruses, catarrh. A few did satiric pantomimes,
two strummed guitars.

Some were Easterners, some lived in the West.
One was a glutton, one wore multi-colored vests.
Others tuned pleasantries and sucked in breath.
Some dismissed their traumas and extolled death.
Some admired wet suit local surfer asses.
Others lusted after bikini-clad lasses.
All believed poetry obdurate: Fame
could arrive early, but would probably come late.
Some sentimentalized mud huts, tepees, and old farms.
Most despised Yuppie fashions and false alarms.
Some shed evidence that their hair lines were receding.
Others loaded the washer and set it spinning.
Some shifted furniture and repositioned pictures.
Most loved gossip and giving mini poetry lectures.
Some gave us cognac, carnations, and wine,
nests of Russian dolls, and jangling tectonic chimes.
All feared cancer, claxons, auto wrecks, and AIDS.
Most despised flatulence, bad reviews, and charades.

We welcomed them all to our home by the sea,
fed them dips, thick roasts, fish, and imported brie,
had guests, soirees, and much conversation,
dissuaded those intent on ejaculation,
pumped up their egos, diminished their libidos,
fluffed their eiderdown, bolsters, and pillows,
served them strong coffee, oatmeal, and bacon.

A POET FROM TUCSON produced a pimply boy to screw.
She'd bought him new Levis, scrubbed him new,
smeared kama sutra oil on his adolescent scrotum,
joy jelly on his cock, and raspberries on his bottom.
(He would enact the X-rated lines as she wrote 'em.)
Since he was sub-literate, there'd be little talk.
She vowed to fuck him until he couldn't walk.
Alas, on the flight down, her menses struck
which meant that she settled for jerking him off.
Her reading was stellar, rife with tears and pluck.
She proclaimed her life a rubber fuck.

A HULKING MID-WESTERNER of substantial fame
sat snivelling on our couch—we wondered why he came.
He'd abused his father and so
had embarrassing pap-smears of guilt to show.
He was sixty, a plump poet-gopher and modest failure
who hoped we'd be his censor and jailer.
His lips turned dour with simulated grief
as he ripped from his genitals the whole fig leaf.
How the critics abused him!
Other poets reviled him!
He'd read his poems, but knew we'd "hate" them.
I rose, kicked open the door, and ejected him.

ANOTHER'S young husband turned flamingly gay.
"Ingrid Bergman you are not," he averred, swishing away.
He wore Cuban heels and parrot green shoes.
His wife, composed, sat at our table,
vowing she should have married Clark Gable.
Dressed in gilt oranges and razor blades
she crossed the Delaware with the King of Spades,
with a nun in a snowmobile traversed Minnesota
and extolled a crock of olives in South Dakota.
Said a young man with pliers, camera, and shears:
"After I load your appliance, let's drink a few beers."
They married (he'd been working at Sears), and
no matter how far-flung their peregrinations,
she, especially, remains irredeemably Californian.

A WATERMELON SOUL with a rubbery paunch,
a miserable pancreas, and an inflamed liver,
meandered the dry Santa Ana river.
Then, after much booze and a halcyon snooze
he insisted I drive him in my car
to a notorious Los Angeles hustler bar.
Though proclaiming (how sad) that he was "hetero,"
he lusted for youths to grope, pay, and blow.
His eyes clouded over as he slurred his words —
sex with women was "strictly for the birds."
Soused, he abandoned his West Hollywood jaunt,
wept that in life he was always defeated,
and even as a Dirty Old Man was usually cheated.

THIS ONE THREW his red wig on a chair:
the ungainly mess near the digital clock
resembled the remains of a whipped fighting cock.

45

He climbed into bed, left shit stains behind,
boasted he never drew window blinds,
wished he were still in Amsterdam or Morocco,
claimed he'd once slept with John Paul Belmondo.
His poems were graphically, libidinously gay,
superbly crafted with much self-display.
He loved dingleberries swirled in kum,
and bacon wiped down the crack of a boy's sweaty bum.

THIS ORPHAN'S birth signs struck a childless couple
who craved a mystical son with double
cusps in rare conjunctions.
Rheumy eyes intensified his visions.
With much panache he scarfed Salvadorian dinners.
He also loved tricking, grand opera, and, broke,
tapped Anais Nin for loans for dates with his blokes.
As a lady of verse Languedocian, Chaucerian,
he wore velvet capes, Oscar Wildean, Venusian.
He swam with us stripped in a Beverly Hills pool,
scatalogically remarked on his tadpole tool.
He was kinky and bright, this Ozian soul.
Now, in Heaven, he sports sapphire-laden aureoles.

THIS ONE brought a sweetie from the tundra,
a poet of sorts filled with conundra
who in the throes of making love
shouted "Mush" at his lady lying above.
He missed the chill wastes, and shortly thereafter
returned to penguins, skuas, and the blubber
he'd hung up for curing in his hand-hewn rafters.

THIS EASTERNER with graying beard, large frame,
and scant publication, famed
recipient of numerous slick poetry prizes,
flew in to regale us with his devices

for transmuting verse into platinum and silver.
He read with tedium, his audience was small.
He praised Ashbery, Ammons, Auden, and Donald Hall,
dismissed the Beats as swinishly maudlin,
coughed self-importantly and blared through his nose,
never begging our pardon for being "indisposed."
That night a long-haired, pot-loving, *poète-maudit*,
sweet publisher of hippies, recidivists, and gays,
who swirled through life in a personal blaze,
shared the man's bolster: what polarities of verse
Western and Eastern! The mattress creaked,
the pillows groaned with much sweet moan
and flailings of gonads and penises.

ANOTHER EASTERNER, of Austrian extraction,
whose family had fled Nazi persecution,
middle-aged, gay (though he seldom avowed it),
an establishment purveyor of polished verses
tinged with Sysyphusean sadness and choruses
crammed with life struggles and boring miasmas,
was totally for "culture," eschewing all funk,
overt sex, raunchy diction, and punk.
He hated small mags and alternative presses.
He'd look great in one of Edith Sitwell's brocade dresses.
His predilections for men he sought to conceal.
Yet, attending gay baths, I'm told, was his Achilles' heel.
"Homoerotic," *not* "homosexual," he loved male bodies.
Like the Greeks, he was spiritual, never "soddy."
Youths in his poems were Adonises and Narcissi
boasting gilt penises and Praxitilean latissimus dorsi.

THIS BARD escaped from a madhouse alive.
A brilliant neo-Villon, much maligned,
who fondled the moon-strands dropped from his brain,
endured exo-skeletal and cerebral pain,

had kids of his own and kids spawned by his women.
Here by the beach, in the sand and the surf,
gulls stabbed his eyes and skewered his liver.
When he read translations of Jean Cocteau,
he teased his audience with an olio
of private and public imbroglios
accompanied by tweets on an old clarinet.
Next day (the weather was stormy and wet)
he hopped a bus to the Mexican border
to see if police had his papers in order
for retrieving his old auto impounded there,
a disorder of piston rings and tappets
abandoned on an earlier visit.

A VIVACIOUS WOMAN of Pulitzer fame
who loved martinis and casual dress,
Fanny Stevenson, raunchy humor, and jests,
gave throaty, vibrant public readings,
and clobbered poets both minuscule and gargantuan
with satire, style, and scathing perceptions.
She wore my pajamas and drank coffee stiff.
Few poets so vibrant had ever hit town
with so coruscatingly personal a merry-go-round.

Wearing ox-blood boots, suede pants,
and much brocade, THIS LADY
sat on our patio and confessed, dismayed:
it had been too long since she'd been laid.
She was a reincarnation of Anäis Nin,
a friend and Bohemian semi-twin
in matters sexual, creative, feminist.
One mauve chapbook and a slim twist of tales
she parlayed into triple NEAs
and numerous visiting writer stints.

Sitting erect – faun-colored hair concealed
her face – she reordered her tendrils,
pressed two fingers beneath her nostrils,
and with two other fingers tapped her caul-spot –
two streaming "life-dots,"
generating synergized axons and ions,
genetical gazelles and Assyrian lions,
recharged her aura, very "bio-energetic,"
holistic, curative, and, hopefully, kinetic.

THIS CHARMER
was enamored of Japanese gardens and delicate vines,
cherry blossoms, jasmine, hibiscus, and eglantine,
waterfalls tinkling like chimed jewelry boxes,
bonsai trees, fairy mushrooms in a ring,
polished stones in the shape of loaves upended.
He wandered, changing his hue from yellow to mauve,
from green to gold, maligned no poets,
barked like a fox, whinnied like a stallion,
gave me a Scythian medallion,
growled like a lion, and sniffled like a grampus.
He was Billy the Kid, the Tooth Fairy,
a Nova, and Captain Gorgeous.
He recited Surrey, Wyatt, Shelley, Spenser, and Blake:
"OH BREAK UP THE FORMS AND FEEL NEW THINGS."
With us he traversed the Bolsa Marsh,
found the pumping oil wells harsh,
asked for a wolf-fur throw for his bed,
slept with a Japanese pillow under his head,
said he would snag the red bomb of the sun.
This he could do better than anyone.

As SEX-KITTEN of the little 'zines,
she drops chapbooks of anorexial extremes,
like a bunny in perpetual parturition.

For originality, she has little competition.
She wears little-girl frocks of pastel hue
accented with sashes of baby blue.
Her Nancy Sinatra boots have class.
She's a mix of the tough and the life-tossed.
Her knees evoke a little girl lost,
her patellas visible in pads of fat.
Her slim legs are apostrophes or commas,
her strophes as slender as her girlish traumas
apt for a madonna teasingly posed
in compromising life and sex positions.
Blonde tresses cascade along her cheeks,
reach to her hips, concealing creeks
of mascara and maquillage.

CODA

Hello, says the pear. Greetings, says the plum. Hi,
says the kumquat. So long, say the persimmon and the
quince.

We plump the eiderdown and freshen the sheets,
burnish our smiles and marinate the roast,
wash dinner plates and polish the silver,
arrange sprays of roses and amaryllis.
Is the new guest Jonathan or is it Phyllis?

Paul, please perk the coffee.

HER MAJESTY
   (for Edith Massey)

The old queen clipped asparagus
and yellow roses to her shoulder
before pitching a moire
ribbon of state over her
obscene bosom.

"Off with their heads!"

To say more is to equivocate.
To say less is to renege.

To be sure, royal words reflect
a ferret's consonants —
whence comes the ermine
she winds lasciviously
around her varicose loins.
Her sybaritic verbals, plosives,
syntactical delights, are
greased silver goblet stems.

We love our queen.
If she's a silvery conflagration
what then of your reputation?

THE WITCH OF THE TOY SHOP

She gutted all the dolls,
The Witch of the Toy Shop.
She drilled their eyes with silver augurs,
dug cedar dust from their heads with a silver spoon,
scattering the excess over her garden
of henbane, night shade, and lurid mushrooms.
She bit off their plastic arms,
crisped their leather toes in candle-flame,
pencilled on genitals (male and female),
then poured on catsup thinned with beet juice.
"All this", she chortled,
"comes from within, from my hot corpuscles.
"I won't have to do a thing," she said.
"Not a thing."

ELDERLY DYING AIDS VICTIM

A man with croup, pneumonia, and bed sores
cuts strings of boy dolls from newspaper,
variously colored.

The boys chant: "We can't any more.
We won't come."

He's trapped inside a urine jug.
The sky glimmers through a magenta window.
A peach-toned hibiscus expires.
Snapping sounds, as though the petals (bacon)
are sizzling.

Flat on his back (those heinous carcinomas)
he beats time on the silly paper boys
dispersed over his chest.

A dirge evokes dragonfly wings clapping,
a hint of a Berlioz (or Verdi) Requiem.

He sees a bronze wall (Ashurbanipal's):
boys as gilt angels assemble
along a glowing coppery fissure.
Into this he slips, without bread,
without a sigh, into death's meal.

FRUSTRATION POEM

On the clangorous steppes of Tibet
against Mongols in furs, with drawn scimitars,
a circuitous illusion
spins round a central ring.

This is a circus.
This is hibiscus.
This is opalescent water.
Sing to the ponies. Sing to the herds. Sing to the
babies.

THE INVUNCHE AND THE DEFORMER

(This poem is based on a passage in Bruce Chatwin's
In Patagonia.)

1.

Our abducted child
is far more repulsive than Satan-talk disgorged
through a lanced fontanelle.

Dear reader, you may be glad you came.

2.

The male cult would have it so,
and has, since Europeans
washed ashore here
miserable in the gales.

These jagged mountains,
storm-smitten, resound
with insane cachinnations
cowing us
on these paper-thin strands,
near a fire of dried guano,
gnarled cypress twigs,
sloth bones, goat knuckles,
sandal-wood, mink viscera.

Naked arm to thigh, we fashion
irregular parallelograms
while chanting diapasons.
Ghosts rot in puddings concocted
of imagoes and butterflies.

3.

Life's brummagem, mass killers,
screeching owl claws,
snakes writhing,
gobbets of carrion—
greed.
Angels rend their pinions.

4.

Fiery black sand
spits forth a child
writhen, whisked
from a gilt cherub sleigh.
I am his Deformer.

5.

He lies on chipped marble.
Watch him burble and suck his little fist.
He's eaten locust porridge
laced with urine and mare's milk.
His playmates are a spiny echidna
and a leashed bull frog.

I tickle his feet.
His fingers are fat grubs, milk-veined,
as translucent as his skull-skin.

We feed him pap sweetened with honey,
a black cat's milk, and crystallized sugar.

I dislocate his shoulder. He screams.

He clambers deep into the cave, with the toads,
where he curls, shuddering.

6.

A full moon at the trine.
Saturn in Venus:
the greater the initial deformity
the more startling the shape,
hence, the more revelatory.

7.

He's naked, on a warm stone
smeared with saffron oil.
His buttered leg twists.
The femur slides.
Cartilage snaps.
No blood, externally at least.
A few days of swelling, some hemiplegia.

A leather bag covers his head.
I slice a figure 8 in his shoulder,
staunch blood (the flow is minimal).
I insert his tiny hand,
sewing it in with ram sinew.

His body is a carapace.
He's dropped by an eagle,
a squiggle on the turf, with tentacles.

I rotate his skull:
By seeing only what lies behind
he'll know this dismal world.
In Hell he won't pick roses.

Prayers and cups of semen.
We write on parchment, which we later burn.
Salmon-tinged smoke masks the cave's mouth.
Putrefaction. The whiff we require.

Fulgurating air claps violently.
Boulders seal the cave
where we were, where he lies.

SISTER NELL

Roisterous, strapping Nell
in her recycling center
in below zero weather,
a slippery over-hang of snow,
six-foot icicles.
Her space heater puffs, toasting her feet.
Her chair lacks slats.
Mice scurry behind the cardboard partition
and the cavernous bins of green and brown bottles
in freight car loads.
Flattened aluminum cans.
An acre of glass and metal.
"It's a living," she says.

The owner, in Michigan,
dumps the scrap-filled semis onto a barge.
He never pays the promised wage.
Nell threatens to burn the warehouse down.
"I'm like Dad," she boasts. "He sorted junk, too."

She wears Dad's old plaid coat.
She recites his jokes, wears gum boots,
carries a sheathed hunting knife,
pins topless calendar girls
among the invoices, cubic weights.
She whips most of the VFW at pool.
She's the only woman in America
to command a Legion post.
"You're something else, Paul," she says.
"Glad brother Bob brought you along.
Take a seat."

ENRAGED WOMAN

The woman obsessed with jigsaw puzzles
crammed the washer with Nell's clothes,
set the machine whirring,
slashed a floral living room couch,
wrote she was returning to Missoula, Montana.

Earlier, on our Thanksgiving visit
Frieda wouldn't talk, either
because she'd been a nurse
or was despised as a lesbian drunk.

She'd wheeled in furniture, her TV, and clothes,
intending to stay forever, so she averred.
She failed to tell my sister of her cancer,
and that she hated sex.

My job was to roast venison,
hers to furnish tomato sauce, onions, cheese, and
beans.
She had tallow-colored curls and razor lips.
She would pour salt down your throat.
She fiddled her own tunes.

Normally, we'd have stayed in Nell's house.
We rented a rustic motel.
It snowed the morning we left.
We imagined Frieda's boots
circling the car, casting charms.
A ten-pronged buck was foraging grasses:
pristine snowy forest vibrations
(where I was born), deliquescent speech,
a tamarack copse, skittering chickadees.
We've not been back.

THANKSGIVING DAY, 1989

1.

My mother greets me under a eucalyptus
in a barrio park in Santa Ana
for a free turkey dinner.
She's dissolved her halo, converted
her flowing gauze, Heaven-gown
to a day-glo pants suit
and has clamped her teeth back in.

"Being a ghost," she says, "and hence
lacking electrified synapses
I can stab my old face
with fork tines and not feel a thing.
My instep never itches
and my arteries are now free
of globular, rock-hard bacon fat.
I'm better off,
although you're only three years
younger than I was when I died,
and you've already outlived Pa by two.
I wouldn't be here now, but I saw
you weren't invited out for dinner.
None of your kids is coming,
and Paul is attending a dying uncle.
He'll whiff the steaming meat and dressing.
I don't mean to be crude, Son."

"This is no laughing matter," I say.
"If only you'd warned me of your visit."

2.

I found her at 5 a.m. on our porch,
in a patio chair, smoking a Doral,
waiting for the sun to rise
and hummingbirds to sip our roses.

"I'd have made a fruit cake," I said,
"stuffed a goose with chestnuts,
whipped up your favorite pie,
pumpkin or pecan, concocted
from Eagle Brand milk and brown sugar."

Going to the barrio seemed the best solution,
although she demurred: "Won't those brown
folk resent us?" On a rare visit I'd driven her
to Tia Juana to observe the indigents
colorized by merchants for enticing
gringo shoppers. She'd never
forgotten a small girl without panties
who squatted near her fruit-selling mother,
hiked up her skirts and urinated blood.
I'd dropped two quarters in the girl's palm
without ever touching her skin.
"Our poverty in Wisconsin was never this bad,
We always, as dad bragged,
had the proverbial pot to piss in."

3.

White ladies and bearded men
fetch turkey, dressing, cranberries,
peas, celery, carrot sticks, and yams.
The servers poise behind folding tables
covered with cheap turkey-motif paper.

Tri-partite paper plates separate
the cranberries from the peas.
A tape sizzles music by "The Chipmunks."
The families get in line—we go to the rear.
Most fathers wear jeans.
Mothers wear bright scarves.
"Look," mom observes, "the broader their asses,
the tighter the pants." Girls wear frilly
communion dresses. Boys sport casual clothes.
Assorted destitute whites. Emaciated
bearded men in smelly trousers.
Dogs race under the tables.

4.

Mom masticates her dinner with eclat, though
she does complain about the pies, deeming them
the sort churned forth by cheap supermarket
bakeries. The crust, which she leaves on her plate,
resembles wet sea sand. She loves the pecans
in their butterscotch sauce
and stuffs a slab of turkey breast with same.
I can tell she's a ghost,
for the food floats off her fork
into her toothless mouth—no chewing,
no gullet gymnastics.

Later, I follow her to a slimy pond
befouled by coveys of slithering wood ducks.
"They're as obnoxious as snails," Mom says.
"You can't eat 'em, and the conservationists
won't let boys torture and kill 'em. Look,
they keep those lovely mallards away."

She flings bits of potato, meat, and pie
to the latter. I'm nervous, for signs forbid
feeding the water fowl, a misdemeanor.

5.

Late afternoon. The fog rolls in,
though we are three miles from the beach.
Mom shivers. "I wasn't dressed for this."
I take her hand. "I'd like to see the ocean, Son.
I may not come again."
She reassumes mystical attire.

We drive to the storm-damaged municipal pier.
She exits the car. "Wait, Mom."
My voice is so subdued
I feel reverberations rather than hear them.
"It's time," she says, kissing my forehead.
I let her hands drop. "A good day, Son."
I say how much I've missed her.
A wheeling cloud suggests Beethoven's cranium.
Then, there's an art deco gourmet restaurant.
Misty angel figures raise gold goblets.
What are they singing?
"Mom! Mom!"

A SENSIBLE OBSERVATION, A SENSIBLE QUESTION

Let's, I say, devour
Portuguese men of war
broiled with smoked calamari.

A gray lighthouse blinks
as a purple dolphin careens
through a lurid sexual stream.

What a storm! Wet funeral chrysanthemums
bob and toss. I fear
a cortege of outraged sea horses.

"A fine sense of fun,"
says a witch sporting a gardenia.
"Your body's camber tells me that.
So does your bitten tongue.

"You need an intellectual slave,
a tenor, bass, or a boy soprano.
You know the kind I mean.
Don't marry another poet though."

I wave her off.
Obviously, as Jack Spicer wrote,
the grail is mine, obviously.

CHILDHOOD LAKE, BOAT, AND VORTEX

A weather beaten row boat
on a Wisconsin lake.
The rower (he dips the oars)
is about to write a final sentence.
He's adolescent again.
Hiram Ewald who owned the farm is dead.
They had groped one another on Halloween
(he was thirteen) concealed under a pile of logs.

The boat oscillates,
a perfect V concentrically
tied to another boat, semi-visible
in the muck,
recumbent skeleton sans liver spots,
sans ossifying knee cartilage,
sans calcified skulls of parents
and dead infant son.
It's his birthday. He's sixty-seven.

Lacy ghosts flicker from the cranberry bog.
Cars rattle over the rusted bridge heading north.

ENGLISH PULPITS

Note: The pulpits appearing in this poem are in obscure English village churches of the sort not frequented by American tourists. Whether or not the reader is aware of these specific sites is irrelevant: the poem is meant as a testament of friendship from one poet to another. These visits with Paul Trachtenberg occurred in the summer of 1987; Janine Dakyns accompanied us. The effect here would be similar to writing a poem on Tierra del Fuego, remarking on salient stops, as Bruce Chatwin did in *In Patagonia*. Few American readers would, of course, have ever seen southern Argentina. Regard these remote, small churches as vicarages of the mind. An earlier version of the complete work appeared in *The Signal* (Nov. 1990).

PRELUDE

But Jesus dies and comes back again with holes in his hands.
    Like the weather.
And is, I hope, to be reached, and is something to pray to
And is the Son of God.

                    —Jack Spicer, "Four Poems for Ramparts."

The pulpits were often redundant,
so ancient (as at Bungay, Snowshill, and Salle).
The medieval wall pictures glimmered
as mere ghosts with hands upraised
or folded behind you.
God, there, seemed palpable.

67

You were, I suppose, heretical.
A bishop would have died hiccuping had he seen
your irreverent benedictions, or he would have
unleashed the black panther, that medieval beast
with breath so sweet he lures sinners to his feast.

Yet, you believe in God, a figure
I suspect, although I've seen the sky
crammed with weeping astronauts, gilt
angels and bright Hephaestuses on flights
of mercy and enterprise,
and I have prayed, at times, in ecstasy,
and at others because I was afraid.
Why God bothers, if indeed He does,
remains obscure.

I.

At St. Ives the morning was blustery.
Victorian clover leaves adorned
the pulpit, red prayer books on the communion
rail, golden staffs to either side, a lectern
cloaked in embroidered tapestry,
a soaring stone arch, someone's baroque
funeral plaque.

Your palms faced outward, gardenias
flowering in snow, gentians,
meadow black-eyed susans, the lectern
a water-lily unfolding in a storm.
Later, on the beach, hotcross buns
and the American poet
married to her Cornish fisherman.

II.

At Truro, climbing was risky,
for a nosey verger was suspicious.
The golden pulpit was ten feet tall,
adorned with images in a swirl,
resembling one of Queen Victoria's
ornate dinner compote holders. A magnificent
golden eagle spread its wings to support
a buckram Bible. Candelabra encrusted
with gilt and fruited vines. Four gold
ewer-bearing maidens, one for each corner
of the universe. Lower, a weighted pedestal
sufficient for supporting Heaven.

This time, hands in pockets
you peered towards an enormous white wax candle,
your hair absorbing color from the eagle's wing.
You could not read the fine print of the spiritual
contract, and, smiling, delayed kisses
for a later chapel. Cathedrals, after all, being grand,
induce uneasiness.

Less formal was the church at Deal,
as plain as the name, honey-colored oak,
an efficient reading light over the lectern.

A silver pipe organ thrust deep
into the well of the apse.
A warm excrescence of panelling
drew up harmonious laughter, a holy soup
of bourdons. The organ stops throttled
a mighty, silent fugue.

III.

Lostwithiel,
refuge in a storm. The tiny railway platform.
The swift excursion through the town.
A pulpit of carved black oak
adorned with black roses and leather
gothic arches. Poised between two simple pews
complete with wine-colored kneeling boards
you clenched the pulpit rim, staring
towards the vestry door, amazed...
or were you merely censorious
snagged by the dour crucifix on the wall
and the mullioned window filled with fractured light,
to your right?

IV.

At Snowshill an old museum
was crammed with farm tools, clocks, swords, and
cheap orientalia. Ancient St. Eadburgh
contained a catafalque on wooden wheels
(once loaded with plague victims).
I tried it for size.

The pulpit, a simple octagon of oak carved
with vines, sat on a base of stone
extruding from an ascending pillar. Clad
in a thermal blue shirt you looked up
from the open book, raised your hand
receiving gospel news.
The watch on your right wrist
was in character, a comma out of place,
appropriate here but not for the next world.

V.

At Bungay
white stone and badly faded medieval paintings
of the apocalypse. An anemic lectern
covered with a pea green cloth, to the side
as though facing mice rather than parishioners.
A modern lamp with a plastic white shade.
The pulpit itself was open-carved, ie.,
your legs were visible through the interstices.

I lit a candle for each of my children
then held my fingers in the flames.

VI.

We're on the Tynwold
that ancient Celtic seat on the Isle of Man
backdrop of a hill
down which they rolled witches sealed in barrels.

Inside the squat museum/chapel
photos of pompous flags, men in white wigs,
a prime minister, a frumpy queen.

A grail floats over a flock of sheep
sprouts wings and elevates.
Medieval space object drips silver blood,
spewing incense.

A joust for dead folk: knights and ladies
who've shed their wimples,
an archbishop of skulls,
urchins tossed in for local color.

71

VII.

At Stanton where young John Wesley
preached, much simplicity. A lady
arranged bouquets and felt she was
intruding. The pulpit adjoined
a black carved altar screen
behind which shone a painted crucifix
in an early Italian style.
The lady led us to the organ loft
to consider the pipes and the magnificent
fourteenth century struts and timbers.
We stood gazing down, ready to welcome
a wedding party, a godfather holding
a godson in his arms.

VIII.

At Helpston where poet John Clare's remains
remain, another drizzling day.
Kneeling-stools with bright
crosses, stars, and angel wings,
one for each pew, at eye level,
a parish ladies' project for hallowing
the church with colored wool.
A verger's gilt wand. A snap-on pulpit light.
To the left a banner: "Show Them Jesus"
and a small teal altar set with candles
behind a golden drape.

You are about to launch a eulogy
on John Clare's sheep crook. On
his fractured brain. His badger
carnaged by village hounds and bullies.
Our departure for home.

CODA

Ascending old pulpits is
to drink from communion cups
rinsed with raspberry juice.
To embellish fine points of verse,
lessons for the day, to catch tomb
and graveyard thrums. Old Tiddles
the church cat scratches his coffin lid.
Cheeping sparrows, rooks, magical,
resonating in these obscure sanctuaries.
Our lives.

HE PREPARES FOR HIS DEMISE

You fear that my plumb bob, slide rule,
compass, and astrolabe
will slice you into
money certificates and impossible mutual funds.
You've played too long
with Lincoln Logs and Erector sets.

Here I fail.
A ferris wheel collapses,
a windowless cabin, a crumbled trestle.

Accompanied by muscle men
I descend purple stairs.
I dismiss my servants.
My former wife has married an emphysemiac.
I still expect a major literary prize.

Here's a simple urn for my ashes.
I think I'm Doctor Phibes.
I'll order a quintet of white mice
to scrape viols and bang funeral tambourines.
The scarlet smear on my throat
is commemorative, death's
ambassadorial slash.

Be kind.
Note the jouncing withers of the black horse
drawing my catafalque. Throw me a top hat.
Don't slam me to the cement.
I wish I'd been the carpenter my father wanted.

Eventually, when the furnace knocks, bangs,
and croaks, seal my eyes.
Perfume my navel. File my nails to points.
Carve *finis* across my chest.
Insert peacock feathers in my ears.
Cremate me.
Char the purple smirk on my lips.

OTHER BOOKS BY ROBERT PETERS CAN BE ORDERED DIRECTLY
(Most are Out Of Print)

THE POET AS ICE-SKATER
    Anthology of poems to Whitman, Lorca, Ginsberg, Jack Spicer, Goethe, and Arthur Rimbaud. Out of print.
Manroot Books, 1976.   Paper $10.00

GAUGUIN'S CHAIR: NEW AND SELECTED POEMS
    Selection of poems, including the poet's much-praised elegy, *Songs For A Son*, and a seminal interview. Out of print.
Crossing Press, 1977.   0-912278-74-9   Paper $10.00

THE DROWNED MAN TO THE FISH
    Poems commemorating marriage breakup and moving to a gay life.
New Rivers, 1978.   0-898230-02-0   Paper $7.00

WHAT JOHN DILLINGER MEANT TO ME
    Poems about the maturing gay psyche on the Wisconsin farm. Out of print.
Sea Horse Press, 1983.   0-933322-09-7   Paper $10.00

MAD LUDWIG OF BAVARIA: POEMS AND A PLAY
    Much-heralded poetic treatment of the life of a homosexual king. Out of print.
Cherry Valley Eds., 1984.   0-916156-82-6   Paper $7.00

HAWKER
    Verse biography of the very eccentric vicar, mystic, and poet, Stephen Hawker. Out of print.
Unicorn Press, 1985.   0-87775-165-X   Cloth $20.00
                         0-87775-166-8   Paper $10.00

KANE
Verse portrait of Elisha Kent Kane; men struggling for survival in the Arctic wastes. Out of print.

Unicorn Press, 1986.   0-87775-468-4   Cloth $20.00
0-87775-169-8   Paper $10.00

THE BLOOD COUNTESS: POEMS AND A PLAY
Story of the notorious 17th century lesbian mass murderer. Out of print.

Cherry Valley, 1987.   0-916156-80-X   Cloth $15.00
0-916156-81-8   Paper $9.00

SHAKER LIGHT
Poems about the Shaker experience in America under the mystic Ann Lee. Out of print.

Unicorn Press, 1988.   0-87775-200-1   Cloth $20.00
0-87775-201-X   Paper $10.00

CRUNCHING GRAVEL: ON GROWING UP IN THE THIRTIES
Memoir of life in rural poverty and of the author's homosexual stirrings. Out of print.

Mercury House, 1988.   0-916515-34-6   Cloth $20.00

HAYDON
Poems about the struggles for recognition and the suicide of the famous Victorian painter and author. Out of print.

Unicorn Press, 1989.   0-87775-219-2   Cloth $20.00
0-87775-220-6   Paper $10.00

(We pay the sales tax.)

Book Sub-Total   US $ _____

Add $2.00 per book for shipping   US $ _____

($4.00 for overseas)   **TOTAL US $**

Send check or money order (no credit cards or phone orders, please) to:

GLB Publishers
P.O. Box 78212, San Francisco, CA 94107